With special thanks to Lucy Courtenay and Nellie Ryan.

First published in Great Britain by HarperCollins *Children's Books* 2009
HarperCollins Children's Books is a division of HarperCollins*Publishers* Ltd,
77-85 Fulham Palace Road, Hammersmith, London W6 8JB

The HarperCollins *Children's Books* website address is
www.harpercollins.co.uk

1

Dream Dogs : Crystal
Text copyright © HarperCollins 2010
Illustrations copyright © HarperCollins 2010

ISBN-13 978 0 00 7320370

Printed and bound in England by
Clays Ltd, St Ives plc

Dream Dogs

CRYSTAL

Aimee Harper

HarperCollins *Children's Books*

Special thanks to
The Happy Dog Grooming Parlour, Farnham

Introducing...

Name: Crystal

Breed: Pomeranian (Pom)

Age: 1

Colour: Creamy butterscotch and snowy white

Likes: Playing outside, kisses and cuddles

Dislikes: Her diamante collar

Most likely to be mistaken for: A teddy bear

Least likely to be mistaken for: A muddy Great Dane!

One

Here is The News

Bella put her head out from behind the changing-room curtain. "Are you ready, Mum?" she said in excitement.

Bella's mum, Suzi, put down the magazine she had been reading. "Come on then," she said. "Show us what you've found."

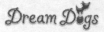

Bella flung back the curtain. The silky t-shirt fell to her knees and the fabric felt really light and lovely on her skin. But the best bit of all was the big picture of a puppy on the front. The puppy was panting in the cutest way. All around the picture was a frame of sprinkled sequins that caught the shop lights.

Bella's little brother, Louie, stuck his fingers down his throat and pretended to throw up.

Ignoring him, Bella gazed hopefully at her mum. Suzi ran a dog parlour called Dream Dogs in Sandmouth, where they lived. She was completely crazy about dogs, just the same as Bella was. She was bound to *love* this outfit. Wasn't she?

"What do you think?" Bella prompted. "It's for Amber's birthday, remember — down at the beach. I can wear it over my cozzie if it's hot and I can wear it with jeans if it's cold."

"It's GROSS!" Louie hooted.

Bella looked scornfully at her brother in his grotty old Sandmouth Hornets football shirt. She wondered if Louie ever actually took his shirt *off.*

"Like you're a fashion expert," she said. "NOT."

At last, Suzi reacted by bursting into laughter. Bella wasn't sure if this was a good thing or not. She waited cautiously until her mum stopped spluttering

"I love it!" Suzi gasped. "Do they have it in my size? Oh, you have to get that for the party, Bella, love. It's completely *perfect.*"

Louie groaned. Bella shot him a triumphant glance and whisked back into the changing room again to take it off. She could have it! She'd be the best-dressed girl at Amber's beach party for sure!

"I saw something like this in one of your magazines, Mum," Bella said happily as they went up to the till to pay for the new t-shirt. "Mimi Taylor was wearing it."

Taking out her purse, Suzi counted the money for the girl behind the till. "I remember," she said. "Only Mimi had it quite tight and cropped, didn't she?"

"With a cute picture of her little dog, Crystal, on the front," Bella said with a sigh. "She got it done specially. Crystal goes *everywhere* with Mimi. I wish we could take Pepper anywhere *we* wanted."

Bella, her mum and her brother all looked out of the shop. Pepper, their scruffy brown dog, was sitting patiently on the pavement with his lead tied to a post by the door.

"I bet Mimi can take Crystal into shops," Bella continued.

"Mimi carries her little dog in a special bag," Suzi pointed out. "I don't think Pepper would like that very much. Besides, he'd be much too heavy to carry around all day. I'd feel like I was lugging the supermarket shopping everywhere I went."

Louie looked disgusted. "The only interesting thing about Mimi Taylor," he said, "is that she's married to *Idaho* Taylor."

Suzi looked blank.

"The footballer, Mum," Bella reminded her. Her mum was well up on fashion icons, but not on who they were married to.

"Oh yes," said Suzi, nodding. "He plays for Chelsea United or something, doesn't he?"

As Bella and Louie both rolled their eyes, Bella heard the girl behind the till clearing her throat. She was doing it in this special way which Bella knew at once meant that she wanted to say something important.

"Excuse me butting in," said the girl, "but I don't suppose you've heard yet, have you?"

Suzi's eyes brightened. She could smell gossip a mile away. "Heard what?" she said at once.

The girl took her time folding Bella's new

t-shirt and sliding it carefully into the bag. "About Mimi Taylor," she said, pushing the bag towards Bella.

"What about her?" Bella asked. For some reason, her heart had started thumping. There was something in the girl's face.

"She's moving to Sandmouth," said the girl triumphantly. "Her boyfriend's just been bought by the Hornets."

Louie choked.

"Sandmouth Hornets have bought Idaho Taylor?" Bella gasped out loud.

The girl leaned forward. "My boyfriend works at the estate agent's up the hill," she said in a confiding way. "He's just sold a big house to a footballer who needed somewhere for himself, his wife, his son and his *very small dog*. Idaho Taylor is going to be playing for the Hornets next season!"

Two

Football Crazy

Louie charged out of the shop. "IDAHO TAYLOR!" he yelled. "IDAHO TAYLOR'S GONNA PLAY FOR THE HORNETS!"

Suzi dashed out of the shop after him. "LOUIE!" Bella heard her mum hollering. "LOUIE, come back here!"

Bella tried to gather her scattered thoughts. Mimi Taylor! Here in Sandmouth! It was unbelievable!

"I'm really sorry my brother's yelling like that," she said to the girl behind the till. Words and thoughts were tumbling through her head like a rockfall. "I hope it wasn't meant to be a secret!"

"It was until this morning," said the girl cheerfully. "But nothing stays a secret in Sandmouth for long. It'll be in the paper today, I expect. But don't forget — you heard it here first!"

Outside the shop window, Bella could see that her mum had caught Louie and was now scolding him. Louie was hopping up and down like a rabbit on elastic but he had stopped shouting Idaho Taylor's name.

Still in a daze at the news that a mega fashion icon like Mimi Taylor was going to be living in her home town, Bella knelt down to untie Pepper. Pepper jumped up at her, barking madly. Louie's excitement was infectious.

"Mimi Taylor is coming to live in Sandmouth!" Bella said breathlessly, giving Pepper a big squeezy hug that made him yelp. "I can't WAIT to tell Amber!"

Bella skipped the whole way home, the bag with her new t-shirt swinging from her hand. She was meeting Amber at the beach in an hour. She'd tell her about Mimi Taylor then. It would be *great*. She couldn't wait to see the shock on her best friend's face!

"IDAHO," Louie began, swinging round a lamp-post.

"*Louie!*"

"Sorry, Mum..."

Bella skipped after her mum and her brother, down on to the seafront and along the beach. The wind gusted in over the sand, taking away the heat of the bright May sunshine.

"MIMI," she sang. "MIMI! MIMI!"

"Hey!" said Louie indignantly. "How come you're not telling Bella off, Mum?"

"I'm just singing," Bella giggled. "Mimimimimi…"

"That's enough, kids," said Suzi. She looked quite breathless herself. "The first editions of the *Sandmouth Bugle* should be in by now. I wonder if it's got the news?"

Judging from the group of people standing around the news kiosk on the beach, the news was already spreading. Suzi bought a paper, lifting it high out of Louie's reach. IDAHO COMING TO SANDMOUTH! roared the headline.

Pepper barked and jumped up at the paper like it was a bone. Suzi rolled it tightly against the wind and tucked it under her arm.

"We can read it back at home," she said. "Come on. My first appointment today is at ten-thirty, and it's nearly twenty-five past."

"Who's coming?" Bella asked. She hoped it would be someone who'd be as excited as she was about Mimi Taylor.

"Mr Evans," said Suzi. "Barney and Nugget both need a wash and a trim."

Bella gave a whoop. Her teacher Mr Evans

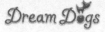

had two golden retrievers. One of them, Nugget, had stayed with Bella for a while until Mr Evans had offered Nugget a permanent home. Now Nugget was one of Bella's favourite customers. Mr Evans wasn't a big follower of fashion though. She'd have to save her news for Amber after all.

Mr Evans was standing outside Dream Dogs as Suzi rushed up to the salon door with her keys.

"Have you heard the news, Mr Evans?" said Louie breathlessly. "Idaho Taylor is coming to play for the Hornets!"

"I know," Mr Evans smiled, "His son is joining Cliffside Primary. Your class, in fact, Louie. I was sworn to secrecy, of course. But now the news is

out, I suppose there's no harm in telling you."

"Idaho Taylor's son is going to be in my class?"

said Louie. He sounded almost hysterical. "My

class?"

"What's the lad called?" asked Suzi, unlocking the salon door and letting everyone in. "Tiger or something, isn't it?"

"Panther," said Mr Evans. "Pan for short, apparently."

Bella giggled. It was a crazy name. But theneverything felt crazy today.

Bella helped Suzi adjust the water temperature in the shower head as Suzi and Mr Evans chatted about the news. Louie raced to the flat, keen to look up all the facts he could find about Idaho Taylor.

"Come on, Nugget," said Suzi, coaxing the golden retriever up the steps that led to the waist-high bath. "Come along now. This won't hurt."

Maybe they'd actually meet Mimi Taylor at the school gates, Bella thought dreamily. She fondled Nugget's ears, and the big golden dog jumped up at her.

"Down, girl!" she laughed, and aimed the shower head at Nugget's shaggy back.

Nugget was very shaggy. It took ages just to get her fur wet enough to lather up the shampoo. She stood patiently as Bella and her mum soaped around her face and under her tummy, round her feet and her tail.

"I wonder if Mimi will bring her

little dog to the salon?" Suzi said suddenly.

"Oooh!" Bella gasped. Dream Dogs *was* the only dog salon in Sandmouth. Mimi and Crystal were bound to visit!

"Oooh!" Mr Evans shouted, but for slightly different reasons. "Be careful where you're pointing that water, Bella!"

Bella lowered the shower head quickly and turned off the taps. She'd just soaked Mr Evans's shoes.

"It's ten past eleven, Bella," said Suzi, checking the clock on the salon wall. "Weren't you supposed to meet Amber on the beach at eleven?"

"Hmm?" said Bella dreamily. She was lost in a daydream where her mum became Mimi Taylor's best friend and she, Bella, got invited round to try on all of Mimi's clothes while her mum and Mimi drank coffee.

"Amber?" Suzi repeated.

Bella dropped the shower head into the bath. She'd completely forgotten. Amber was always on time when they met up. She was going to be *well* mad.

"Gotta go!" she gasped, before grabbing a fleece off the peg by the door and charging out of the salon. "Come on, Pepper. Walkies!"

Three

Surprise at the Salon

It was twenty past eleven before Bella arrived at the place where she and Amber had arranged to meet.

"What time do you call this?" Amber said, folding her arms.

"Sorry," Bella panted. She was out of breath.

Pepper frisked down to the water's edge and started barking merrily at the waves. "But there's been the most amazing news, Amber. You won't believe it, but—"

"Idaho Taylor's going to play for the Hornets, I know," Amber interrupted. "My brother's a Hornets fan too, remember?"

Bella stopped. The girl in the shop had been right. Nothing stayed a secret in Sandmouth for long.

"So you know about Mimi too then?" she said, disappointed. "Mum thinks she'll bring Crystal to the salon! How cool is *that*?"

Amber shrugged. "Whatever," she said. "Listen, now you're here can we talk about the party?"

"What party?" said Bella absently.

"MY party," said Amber. She frowned. "That's why we're meeting, remember?"

Oops. Bella's head was so full of Mimi Taylor that she'd actually forgotten about Amber's party. "Oh yes, of course," she said quickly. "I just bought the best top for the party, Amber.

It's got a puppy on the front! Mimi wore one just like it in the gossip pages a couple of weeks ago, only mine is longer and—"

Amber was starting to look cross. "I don't want to talk about Mimi Taylor," she said. "I want to talk about the *party*. We have to organise beach games and things to do. I can't

do it on my own. You said you'd help. And all you've done so far is go on about Mimi."

Bella tried to focus on Amber's party. She stared around at the patch of beach where they were standing. It was next to one of the groynes that pushed out into the sea and stopped the currents from washing away the sand. "So is this the bit where you're going to have the party?" she said.

Amber nodded, looking a bit more cheerful. "When the tide goes out there's always a really warm pool of water just here. We can swim in it. And Mum suggested beach volleyball," she said. "What do you reckon?"

Bella remembered how she'd seen a picture of

Mimi in the papers last summer playing beach volleyball in a really cute lime-green bikini. She wondered whether she could persuade her mum to get her a bikini like that.

"Earth to Bella?" said Amber loudly.

"Hmm?" said Bella.

Amber threw her arms in the air. "Forget it," she said, and started stomping off. "See you when you've got your brain back."

"Sorry," Bella called after Amber guiltily. "Listen, beach volleyball's a really good idea. You should go with that."

Amber ignored her and kept walking, hands deep in the pockets of her blue hoodie. Bella wondered if she should go after her. But then Pepper barked for her attention, and before you could say "Idaho" Bella was back in Mimi world.

"Let's get back to Dream Dogs," she said, ruffling Pepper's wiry fur and making him squirm with pleasure. "You never know, Mum might have taken a booking from Mimi already!"

Back at the salon, Suzi had just finished hosing

the shampoo off Barney's broad back. Looking

silky and clean and lovely, Nugget sat under the

window seat panting happily. Mr Evans was on

the seat above Nugget, flipping through the

pages of the *Sandmouth Bugle*. From what Bella could see, most of the paper was taken up with Idaho and Mimi Taylor.

"Was Amber still there?" Suzi asked, rinsing away the bubbles.

"Yes," said Bella. She felt guilty as she thought about Amber. "But she wasn't very pleased."

"I'm not surprised," said Suzi. "It's not much fun waiting around."

"All right," said Bella crossly. "There's no need to go on about it. Do you want a hand getting Barney out of the bath, Mum?"

Barney lurched out of the bath, his wet paws scrabbling around as Bella pulled on his collar. Before the big dog could shake himself and soak everyone, Suzi deftly threw a towel across his shoulders and began rubbing hard. Bella had a towel too, and did the same. It was hot work. Barney wriggled free and shook himself, but most of the water had already been rubbed off.

Bella jumped out of her skin as Louie came charging into the salon from the adjoining flat door.

"Mimi..." he panted. "Mimi's coming... Saw her

out of the kitchen window..."

Bella jerked round. Her foot slipped in a puddle of water. She let go of Barney, who bounded down the bath steps with a joyful bark and threw himself at Mr Evans. Suzi shrieked. Mr Evans shouted. Bella went over with an undignified bump on her bottom just as the salon door tinkled and a woman stepped through the door, clutching a tiny little dog in her arms.

Bella gasped for breath. Mimi Taylor's designer sandals tapped over the salon floor towards her.

"Are you OK?" Mimi Taylor asked.

Louie got a fit of the giggles in the corner of the salon. Suzi was trying to wipe Mr Evans's jumper and look at Mimi at the same time, while Mr Evans struggled to get Barney back under control.

"You're Mimi," said Bella stupidly.

Mimi grinned. "Last time I looked, yes," she said.

She held out a slim hand to pull Bella up. Bella could see a foxy little face gazing out from the crook of Mimi's other arm. Crystal the Pomeranian had bright, intelligent brown eyes, and her furry little ears were pricked up. Her fluffy coat was a creamy butterscotch brown all over, except for her snowy white chest and paws.

Louie was still snorting in the corner as Bella slowly got up with Mimi's help.

"It was a puddle," Bella said. Why did everything that was coming out of her mouth sound so stupid?

"I've done that," said Mimi sympathetically. She looked over at Suzi, who had stopped towelling Mr Evans. "Are you the lady who runs this salon?" she asked.

"Yes," Suzi squeaked. She looked like one of those meerkats you see on nature programmes, Bella thought. All alert and wide-eyed and slightly mad.

"Lovely place," Mimi said. She gazed around at the pink walls and green hanging plants. "Pink's my favourite colour."

"Me too," said Suzi and Bella at the same time.

"It's a bit cheeky," said Mimi, "but I wondered if you could fit Crystal in for a shampoo and claw-trim? I'm sorry I didn't call."

Four

Mimi

Suzi recovered first.

"I'm just finishing this one," she said, nodding at Barney. "But I can do Crystal straight afterwards if you don't mind waiting, Mrs Taylor?"

Mimi settled down on the window seat beside

Mr Evans. "That's fine," she said, nuzzling Crystal. "But please call me Mimi. Everyone does."

Louie was still laughing. With a glare, Suzi shooed him back up to the flat. Bella went over and set up the big dog-dryer for Barney. Why couldn't she think of anything to say?

The blasting noise of the dryer drowned any hope of a conversation. Bella rubbed hard at Barney's coat, sneaking little glances at Mimi every now and then. She looked amazing up close. She was really pretty, with thick black hair that hung in a curtain of curls down her back, and huge hazel eyes and what looked like sparkly diamonds in her ears. She was wearing fabulous clothes too. Cropped white jeans, a

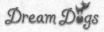

midnight-blue silk top and a long, white waistcoat thing that Bella instantly wanted. On her feet were a pair of strappy leather sandals that showed off her tanned ankles and beautifully French-manicured toenails.

At last, Bella was opening the door so Mr Evans, Barney and Nugget could go home.

"See you on Monday, Bella," said Mr Evans.

"Bye!" said Bella breathlessly. She shut the door and turned back to stare at Mimi Taylor again.

"I'm sorry we haven't got a small bath," Suzi apologised. "But they're very expensive. We can wash Crystal in the basin if you like."

Mimi laughed, a lovely tinkly sound. "She's my

baby, so the basin will be fine," she said. "I used to bath Pan in the basin as well."

"Pan's going to be at my school," said Bella shyly, sitting down beside Pepper's basket and cuddling him.

"That's why we've come to Sandmouth early," Mimi explained. "My husband wants us to settle in before he gets caught up in the new football season."

Bella listened as Mimi talked and her mum shampooed Crystal. The little dog looked even tinier now she was wet. Bella felt like she could listen for hours. Every now and then, she reached out her fingers and Crystal gave her a sniff.

Mimi was in the middle of a funny story about how Idaho had proposed to her when the phone rang. Reluctantly, Bella went over to pick up the receiver.

"Bella? It's Amber. I'm sorry about earlier. I'm just getting stressed about my party because I'm worried about everyone having a good time."

Mimi had just got to the part where Idaho had dropped the ring down a grating in the road.

"Can't talk now," Bella whispered. "Mimi's

here. Mum's washing Crystal. I feel like I'm in a film or something. Can I call you back?"

There was a pause.

"OK," said Amber reluctantly. "I'm going up to my nan's in half an hour, for the rest of the weekend though. Ring me back before then, won't you?"

"Sure," said Bella quickly. Suzi had just burst out laughing at something Mimi had said. "See you."

Crystal didn't take long to wash. Her silky coat was very soft and smooth, and Suzi only used a little hairdryer on her.

"She feels the cold," Mimi explained. "Come on, baby. Let's put on your little jumper, shall we?"

Mimi took a tiny pink cashmere dog wrap with little purple tiaras embroidered on it out of her expensive-looking handbag and wrapped it tenderly round Crystal's shoulders.

Suzi now examined Crystal's claws. "These don't look too bad," she said. "I'll just file them, shall I?"

"Do you have any nail varnish?" Mimi asked. "She looks so adorable when her claws are painted."

Suzi blinked. As far as Bella knew, they'd never painted a dog's claws with nail varnish before.

"No," said Suzi apologetically. "I'm afraid not."

Mimi rummaged around in her bag and produced a little bottle of pink nail varnish. "Here we are," she said triumphantly. "Now, if I hold her could you paint her claws?"

Bella felt strange watching her mum putting nail varnish on Crystal's claws. Nail varnish just wasn't very — *doggie*. Crystal growled and wriggled as Mimi spoke soothingly to her.

"There," said Suzi. "Now, a quick blast of the hairdryer and Crystal can run around outside all she likes without smudging it."

"Crystal never runs outside the house," said Mimi, holding the growling Pomeranian still as Suzi switched on the dryer and directed it at the little dog's newly pink claws. "It's much too dangerous for a small dog. Her pads are incredibly soft, you know. She'd cut herself."

"All dogs need exercise," said Bella before she could stop herself.

"Don't you worry about Crystal, Bella," said Mimi warmly. "I'd never do anything to harm her. She really is my baby. She's the daughter I never had. Idaho and I can't have any more children, you see. So now I have a little baby girl who'll never grow up. It's every mother's dream!"

Bella wondered if her mum wished that she,

Bella, would never grow up. It didn't seem likely. Suzi often said things like "when you're a teenager" and "if you get married".

"Perfect," Mimi was saying, fluffing up Crystal's soft, freshly washed coat and tucking the little dog back under her arm. "Thank you ever so much, Suzi. We'll see you again soon."

Mimi handed over a generous tip as Bella helped her mum ring up the till. And then she swept away.

"Well," said Suzi at last as the door stopped tinkling and Mimi Taylor disappeared from view. "This has been the strangest day of my life."

Bella pushed away thoughts of dogs and nail varnish. She ran to her mum for a hug. Suzi squealed and twirled her round, caught up in the excitement. And then Bella noticed the clock and realised with an awful lurch that more than half an hour had passed since Amber had called. Bella had promised to call her back before Amber left for her nan's.

Bella ran to the phone and pressed Amber's number. There was no answer.

Five

In Trouble with Amber

Bella stopped at the door of her classroom and frowned. Amber wasn't sitting at the table they usually shared with Sophie Olowu. At first Bella wondered if her best friend was late. Then she saw that Amber was sitting with Evie Elliott on the other side of the room. Amber and Evie's heads were bent together and they were giggling about something.

"I don't know what's wrong with Amber," said Sophie. "She went up to Mr Evans as soon as she came in this morning, and the next thing I know she's gone to sit with Evie. Have you had a fight?"

"Something like that," Bella muttered. She'd meant to call Amber back. She honestly had. But it wasn't every day that Mimi Taylor came into your mum's dog salon, was it?

"Hey," Sophie whispered, her eyes shining. "Did you hear about Idaho and Mimi Taylor moving here?"

Part of Bella wanted to tell Sophie about meeting Mimi. But the rest of her was feeling too upset about Amber. So she just nodded.

"And their son's in your brother's class!" Sophie went on. "Louie is really lucky."

Bella thought about Louie and his best friend, Jamie. They never argued about *anything*. "Yes," she said, feeling a bit sad. "He is."

The morning plodded by like an old donkey. Bella kept sneaking glances at Amber, hoping to catch her friend's eye. Amber ignored her.

The sun was bright at playtime. Bella tried not to feel bad at the way Amber ran off with Evie without looking back at her. She sat on a bench and watched everyone playing for a bit. Then she looked around for Louie and wondered what his morning with Panther Taylor had been like.

Lots of kids were clustered around a dark head in the corner of the playground where Louie and his mates usually played. Bella wandered over to take a look. She could hear a boy's voice somewhere in the middle.

"...and I'm well fast like my name, so look out. Who's gonna race me?"

A tall boy with Mimi Taylor's eyes and his dad's dark skin came zooming out of the crowd. Boys charged after him, whooping loudly. Louie was running among them, and so was Ryan, Evie Elliott's brother. Panther Taylor *was* fast. But Louie was faster. She watched as

her brother legged it past the new boy.

"I won!" Louie cheered and punched the air.

Panther Taylor's face screwed up with rage.

He lashed out with his foot and kicked Louie in

the shin.

"Ow!" Louie shouted.

And then Bella lost sight of her brother as the bell rang and everyone surged past her like a wave, on their way back inside.

In the afternoon, Bella tried to make Amber smile at her. She passed her a book. She fetched clean paper and put some on Amber and Evie's desk when Mr Evans said they were going to do a drawing activity. She kept mouthing "sorry" across the room. But nothing was working. Bella was relieved when the bell went and school was over.

She walked with Sophie down the corridor, listening to

Amber and Evie talking about Amber's party. Bella felt guilty all over again. Amber had said she needed her help for the party. And Bella had let her down – twice.

There seemed to be more parents than usual at the school gates. Everyone looked like they'd dressed up in their best clothes. Amber's mum, Claire, who usually wore joggers and hoodies, was wearing high heels.

The parents all turned as a huge 4x4 with tinted windows drove up and parked. Mimi Taylor flung open the car door. Crystal was in her arms, scratching irritably at the twinkly collar round her neck. A twitter of excitement started up among the waiting parents. It was like

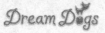
someone had just disturbed a tree full of
sparrows.

Bella waved as Mimi looked
her way. Mimi smiled
back and lifted a dainty
hand to wave back.
Sophie gazed at Bella
in astonishment.

"Did Mimi Taylor just
wave at you?" she said.

"Oh, haven't you heard?" said Amber loudly.
"Mimi and Bella are best friends these days.
Don't waste time with Bella, Sophie. She'll just
drop you like she dropped me."

"I didn't drop you!" Bella said indignantly. "I

just forgot to ring you, OK? I've said sorry a million times today."

Amber glared at her. "Whatever," she said. "Evie's going to do a joint party with me now because it's her birthday too. So I don't need your help any more. And don't bother to turn up on Sunday. Oh, I forgot — you wouldn't have bothered to turn up anyway, would you? Not now you're friends with *Mimi*."

Bella felt her stomach lurch. "You don't want me to come to your party?" she said with dismay.

"No," said Amber, turning to go. "I don't."

By the time Bella found her voice again, Amber and Evie had disappeared into the crowd.

She looked for her mum. To the envy of the rest of the waiting crowd, Suzi was talking to Mimi.

"Will tomorrow be OK?" Mimi was saying. "I'll bring Crystal round at about four. Shaving my initials into her fur is the cutest idea I've ever had."

Bella met her mum's eye and pulled a face. The idea of shaving your initials on your dog was *yucky*.

Panther Taylor marched through the crowd and poked Mimi in the side.

"Pan!" Mimi exclaimed. She gave her son a kiss. "This is my son, Panther," she said proudly to Suzi. "So, love. How was your first day?"

Panther Taylor shrugged. He reached up to

ruffle Crystal's gleaming head. The little dog leaned towards him, closing her big brown eyes with pleasure.

"Don't muss her fur, Pan," Mimi warned, lifting Crystal out of her son's reach. Crystal sneezed and stretched up one of her pink polished claws to scratch at her twinkly collar again.

Bella felt Pepper jumping up against her legs. Bending down she gave Pepper a big hug and breathed in his lovely doggie smell.

"Nice dog," said Pan behind her. "Can I stroke him?"

But before he could bend down and give Pepper a pat, Mimi was pulling him away. Bella watched Panther Taylor slowly climb inside the big car. He looked lonely.

Bella knew how he felt.

Six

A Step Too Far

Bella walked slowly along the beach behind her mum and Louie, listening to her brother complaining about Panther Taylor.

"And then he kicked me, Mum! Talk about a bad loser!"

"He's just new," said Suzi. "He probably thinks

he has to be the best or no one will be friends with him."

Down by the water, Bella could see Amber standing with Evie. They were throwing stones into the waves and laughing. Evie's short blonde hair was blowing around in the wind.

"Why don't you go and talk to Amber, Bella?" Suzi suggested. "This fight all sounds like a silly misunderstanding to me."

Bella knew her mum was right. She walked down the beach towards Amber. She could hear Amber and Evie talking about the party.

"We should put the volleyball net here," Evie was saying, "because the sand's nice and flat so we can run around more easily. And—"

Amber turned round and looked at Bella. "What do you want?" she said.

"I want to say sorry," Bella said.

"It's too late," said Evie smugly. "Amber's friends with me now."

Bella could feel tears coming into her eyes. So she started walking away. "I don't care," she called back over her shoulder. "Mimi Taylor's coming to my mum's salon again tomorrow, and she really likes me, so there."

And then Bella broke into a run because the tears were falling down her cheeks and she really didn't want Evie Elliott to see her crying.

On Wednesday morning before school, Bella did her usual chores in the salon. She straightened the shampoo bottles. She lined up the clean towels. She swept the floor. But none of it was as fun as normal.

Why was I so stupid? Bella thought gloomily. *I should have realised that being friends with Amber was more important than Mimi.*

Bella moved over to the salon pinboard. The board was a Dream Dogs tradition. Photos of Dream Dogs' clients were stuck all over it. It was one of Bella's jobs to straighten the photos and make sure the pinboard looked neat.

The picture of Crystal had been moved from the middle of the board down to the bottom corner. Bella was surprised. Her mum was so proud of her new celebrity client. Why had she moved Crystal's picture?

Louie came into the salon from their adjoining flat door. His school bag swung on his back and he was scowling. "I don't want to go to Pan Taylor's house for a playdate after school," he was grumbling to Suzi. "He'll kick me again."

"Pan wouldn't have invited you if he didn't like you," Suzi said. "It would be unkind not to go."

Louie groaned.

"Why have you moved Crystal's picture, Mum?" Bella asked.

"I've just put a more recent picture of Angus in the middle," Suzi said a bit awkwardly. "Just because Mimi and Crystal have their pictures in the paper sometimes, it doesn't mean we ignore our other dogs, Bella."

"Did you argue with Mimi when she came yesterday?" Bella asked. "About the initials in Crystal's fur?"

Suzi fussed over Bella's hair. "I didn't like doing

those initials," she said at last. "It felt wrong. But I did it and that's that."

"It's a weird thing to do to a dog," said Louie.

Bella agreed.

School was the same as it had been all week. Amber and Evie sat together. Snippets of party plans floated across the room to Bella.

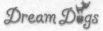

"We can do beach-party makeovers for everyone before the party, Amber!" Bella heard Evie saying.

"I don't think my mum likes me wearing make-up," Amber said.

"Your mum won't mind," Evie said breezily. "We can do it at my house."

Amber glanced over at Bella. Bella pretended she hadn't been listening and scribbled madly in her exercise book.

At the end of the day, Louie went off reluctantly with Pan Taylor in Mimi's huge black car. Bella caught a glimpse of Crystal as Mimi shut the door. The little dog was scratching at her glittery collar again. It looked like Crystal had a sore-looking red ring around her throat, where the collar's sharp edges were rubbing against her skin.

"Crystal's collar is hurting her," Bella told her mum as they walked back home. Pepper scampered around their feet.

"I know," Suzi said. "I pointed it out yesterday, but Mimi assured me that Crystal *liked* her collar and I was making a fuss over nothing."

Bella thought about the nail polish on Crystal's claws and the initials shaved on the Pomeranian's snowy chest. "Mimi isn't a very responsible dog owner, is she?" she said.

"She doesn't mean to be unkind to Crystal," Suzi sighed. "But she treats that dog like a toy.

And I don't know what to do about it."

The Taylors lived in a very exclusive part of Sandmouth. Most of the houses had electric gates. Security cameras winked at them from the top of high garden walls.

"I hope no one arrests us," Suzi joked nervously as they drove up to the Taylors' house to collect Louie.

Bella jumped out of the car for the thrill of pressing the large silver buzzer by the gates. With a gentle hum, the gates swung open.

"Louie's been as good as gold," Mimi said as she opened the huge black front door and smiled at them. Crystal struggled under her arm and barked at Pepper. "They've had a lovely time."

Louie came out, looking relieved to see Bella and Suzi. Pan knelt down and fussed over Pepper. Pepper rolled over and wagged his tail.

"Inside now, love," said Mimi. "And wash your hands. Can't you see that Suzi wants to go home?"

Pan slowly went back into the house. Bella

saw him run towards a football lying in the hall and kick it as hard as he could.

"How many times do I have to tell you, Pan?" Mimi said, spinning round sharply as the ball thudded down the hallway and nearly knocked over a tall Chinese-looking vase. "No balls inside the house! You're as bad as your dad! Honestly," she said, turning back to Suzi crossly. "You've got no idea what it's like, living with boys. If I didn't have Crystal, I'd go mad."

"We'll have Pan tomorrow afternoon, if you like," Suzi offered as Mimi nuzzled her little dog.

Bella heard Louie groan under his breath.

"That would be lovely!" Mimi said. Crystal yapped. "Now, Suzi, have you got an appointment on Friday afternoon? I've had the most fabulous idea about Crystal, and I just know you'll love it."

"What's your idea?" Suzi asked cautiously.

"After her usual wash and blowdry, I want to pierce Crystal's ears!" Mimi said. "Wouldn't she look totally adorable?"

Seven

Friends Again

"Well!" said Suzi crossly as they drove home.
"Now I've heard it all!"

"You're not going to do it, are you, Mum?"
said Bella.

"Of course not!" Suzi spluttered. "Mimi can
bring Crystal round for the usual wash and

blowdry, but that's it."

"Pan kicked me again," Louie said.

Suzi muttered something under her breath. Then she said, "No wonder that boy kicks things. I've never seen anyone more in need of getting tired and dirty. I bet Mimi's never let him jump in a muddy puddle in his whole life!"

Louie looked horrified at the thought of not being allowed to jump in puddles.

"This is the way to Amber's house," said Bella suddenly, recognising the way Suzi was going.

"Yes," said Suzi. "I need to talk to Claire about Snowy's special shampoo she wanted me to order."

Bella's heart bounced around. "Can I wait in

the car?" she asked as Suzi parked and got out.

"Don't be silly, Bella," said Suzi. "We won't be long."

Bella hung around behind her mum as Suzi rang Amber's doorbell. She was half excited and half scared.

"What a nice surprise, Suzi!" said Claire. She kissed Bella's mum warmly on the cheek. "In you come, kids," she said to Bella and Louie. "Joe's upstairs, Louie. And Amber's in the playroom, Bella. She'll be pleased to see you."

"Really?" said Bella cautiously.

Claire smiled. "Of course," she said. "Go and see her. Now, Suzi, about Snowy..."

As Bella walked slowly down the hall, Amber

came out of the playroom. The girls stopped and stared at each other.

"It *is* you," Amber said, and grinned. "Thank goodness for that."

Bella blinked. "So... you're not angry with me any more?" she asked.

Amber shrugged. "You said sorry at the beach, didn't you? I've tried to talk to you a couple of times this week but Evie kept popping up and dragging me away. She's phoned twice this evening already. She's sharing my party and she's trying to take over my life and it's driving me *nuts*."

"I really am sorry, Amber," Bella said honestly.

"I know," Amber said. "So. Wanna play Sims?"

Bella played happily with Amber while Suzi talked to Claire. Everything was back to normal. It felt *brilliant*.

"Bella!" Suzi called at last. "Louie! Time to go."

"I did like Evie's idea about the makeover for our party," said Amber as she and Bella came out of the playroom with their arms linked together. "I just don't think Mum wants me to wear make-up."

"She probably wouldn't mind a bit of glitter and lip gloss," Bella pointed out. "Have you asked?"

Amber shook her head. "I'll ask this evening," she said. "Oh, and Evie's little brother wants to invite Pan Taylor. That would be kind of cool."

"Don't," said Louie at once. "He kicks."

"I kick harder," Amber said with a shrug. "See you at school tomorrow, yeah?"

On Thursday afternoon, Pan came home with Louie, and Amber came home with Bella. As soon as they'd left the school gates and turned on to the beach towards Dream Dogs, Pan was racing for the sea with Louie and Pepper close beside him.

"You promised Mimi you wouldn't let Pan get dirty," Bella reminded Suzi as Pan started splashing Louie and making him yell.

"Did I?" said Suzi. She winked at Amber. "I don't remember."

Louie was now splashing Pan back. Pan looked cross to begin with. But before long, he was laughing and fighting back. Barking like crazy, Pepper was running rings round them both and sending up showers of sand with his paws.

"I'll tell you what," said Suzi. "I don't have any customers this afternoon. Why don't we just stay out here and get fish and chips for tea?"

They spent a lazy hour on the beach, combing for shells and chasing gulls. Bella and Amber

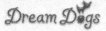

made sand angels. Pan and Louie dug holes and buried each other's feet.

"What did your mum say about the makeover idea?" Bella asked Amber as they dusted the sand off their school dresses and sat together on the sea wall.

"Mum liked it," Amber said. "But we can't do it. Even between me and Evie, we haven't got enough make-up, or enough room for everyone to sit down and have their faces done."

Bella squeezed Amber's arm sympathetically. "Your party will still be really good," she said.

"I guess," said Amber.

Suzi came towards them, carrying fish and chips. Bella, Louie, Amber and Pan all fell on the warm parcels and tucked in while the wind blew their hair around and sand got into the ketchup. Pepper lay at their feet and panted. He was exhausted.

"This is brilliant!" Pan grinned. His face was covered in ketchup. "I never do stuff like this."

"What?" said Louie, stopping mid-chip. "You never have fish and chips?"

"Only on plates," said Pan. "With knives and forks."

"Why does your mum hate you getting dirty?" Bella asked. Vinegar was running down her fingers so she licked them.

"Dunno," Pan said gloomily. "I think she just wishes I was a girl. You should see some of the outfits she tries to make me wear. As if!"

"I'm sure your mum doesn't wish that," said Suzi. "She just doesn't understand what boys need."

"Fish and chips," Louie cheered.

"And water fights!" Amber added.

Pan grinned. "She fusses around Dad too," he said. "So I guess it's not just me. I wish she didn't treat Crystal like a baby all the time, though. I want to play with her sometimes, and I know Crystal wants to. She may be small, but she's dead sparky."

"Have another chip," Bella said, cheekily

dabbing a ketchupy chip on the tip of Pan's nose.

Pan choked with laughter and threw one of his

chips back at Bella.

"Enough!" Suzi shouted, ducking as chips flew

through the air. "Let's get back to Dream Dogs

and put you in the bath, Pan. Otherwise your

mum will have my head on a stick!"

Eight

Makeover Time

"I'm sorry, Mimi," said Suzi. "But I can't pierce Crystal's ears."

It was Friday afternoon. Mimi had arrived with Crystal for her appointment at Dream Dogs, as arranged. From the window seat, Bella watched and held her breath.

"You can't," Mimi demanded, "or you won't?"

"Both," Suzi said. "It's not fair on her, Mimi. I'm sorry."

Crystal yapped under Mimi's arm. "Fine," Mimi said crossly, stroking the little dog. "I'll find someone else to do it."

Suzi shook her head. "No proper dog salon or vet would do such a thing," she said.

Mimi pouted. "I just want my baby to look pretty!" she said.

"She already looks pretty," said Bella. "Honestly she does, Mimi."

Crystal yapped and scratched at her twinkly collar as Mimi's eyes filled with tears. "You don't know what it's like, being the only girl in my house," she sobbed. "Everywhere there's mucky trainers and stinking socks. Crystal's my baby girl!"

"That's the problem," said Suzi. "She's not a baby girl. She's a dog. And although that collar is very pretty, it *is* hurting Crystal. You have to get her something softer."

"Fine," Mimi snapped. "Well, seeing how you think I'm a cruel dog owner, I'll leave, shall I?"

Suzi looked a bit shaky as Mimi marched out of the salon. Bella jumped down from the window seat and gave her mum a big hug.

"You were right," Bella said, looking up at Suzi. "Piercing Crystal's ears would have been all wrong."

"I know," Suzi sighed. "I'm sorry Mimi got upset about it. She's not a bad person, Bella. She's just a person who needs a *lot* of girl-time."

A glimmer of an idea came to Bella. It was so crazy that she dismissed it at once. But then she thought about it again over supper. And again at bath time, and when she got into bed.

Maybe it *would* work. Maybe it was just what everyone needed.

It was raining on Saturday morning. Bella had been thinking about her crazy idea all night. Amber was coming over to play in half an hour. She couldn't wait to test her idea on her best friend.

"It's probably gonna rain for my party tomorrow," said Amber gloomily when she arrived. "And no one will come and it'll be totally awful."

"Don't worry about the weather," Bella said. "Listen to this. What if we asked Mimi if she could do makeovers for your party?"

"You're crazy," said Amber. "Why would Mimi Taylor do that for me?"

"Pan's coming as Evie's brother's guest, isn't he?" Bella said. "Mimi *loves* all the girly stuff. That's why she fusses over Crystal so much. Doing makeovers on twenty girls would be like Mimi's idea of paradise!"

"You're serious, aren't you?" Amber gasped.

"I love it!"

"What are you two planning?" said Suzi, bustling into the salon in a set of pink Dream Dogs overalls.

"The birthday party of the century," said Bella in excitement. And she told her mum all about her big idea.

Suzi was quiet for so long that Bella got worried. Did her mum think it would be too rude, calling Mimi up and asking for such a massive favour?

"It might be just what Mimi needs," said Suzi at last. "And I would like to call her up and see if she's OK. She was so upset yesterday."

Bella high-fived Amber as Suzi went to the phone. The girls listened with baited breath to the conversation.

"Mimi? It's Suzi... I'm sorry about yesterday... what? You do? I'm really glad..."

Bella felt relieved. It sounded like Mimi had forgiven her mum for saying no to the ear-piercing thing.

"I know it's cheeky to ask," Suzi was now saying, "but Amber's having a birthday party tomorrow and we— Oh, Pan's coming is he? Well Bella wondered if you'd consider doing makeovers on Amber's guests before they head for the beach? Only if it's not too much trouble... You would? Oh, Mimi – the girls will be so thrilled. See you tomorrow!"

Bella and Amber were already jumping around and squealing as Suzi hung up the phone.

"She said yes," Suzi smiled. "But I think you worked that out. Didn't you?"

The driveway to the Taylors' house was jammed with cars as mothers dropped off Amber, Evie, Bella and all the party guests for their Mimi makeovers on Sunday morning. The skies were clear, and there was no sign of yesterday's rain. It looked like the beach part of Amber and Evie's party was going to happen after all.

"Come in!" Mimi said joyfully, flinging open the door. Crystal woofed under Mimi's arm. Bella noticed that the Pomeranian had a new, soft pink leather collar round her fluffy neck. "I've got some lovely things lined up. Go through to the conservatory at the back!"

Bella gasped as she, Amber, Evie and the rest of the party guests entered the big glass conservatory beyond the Taylors' kitchen. Mimi had done everything out like a proper beauty salon. There were matching pink chairs lined up

along the big glass table, and little mirrors propped up in front of the chairs. Dotted all over the table were pots of glitter gel, bottles of nail polish, tubes of lip gloss, decorative rubber hair ties in huge glass bowls. There were sheets of stick-on gems for faces and nails, multi-coloured mascaras, hair tongs and rollers and cans of hairspray.

Louie charged out into the garden to play football with Pan and Ryan Elliott as the girls rushed to sit in the pink chairs. Mimi bustled round, offering advice.

"Amber, that lovely pale blue glitter gel will make your eyes look gorgeous... There're four or five different flavours of lip gloss, girls... Does anyone want me to braid their hair? It's a great

beach look..."

As Bella sat down in one of the pink chairs,

she noticed that Mimi had put Crystal down on

the ground. The little Pom woofed with delight

and started chasing her tail.

"This was *such* a great idea, Bella," said

Amber happily.

"Fantastic!" said Evie.

There was a chorus of "Wicked!" and "Fab!" up and down the table.

The front door banged open. Bella nearly choked as Idaho Taylor came into the kitchen, his kit bag swinging from his shoulder. It was the first time she'd seen him up close.

"Dad!" Pan shouted from outside. "Come and play!"

Bella caught sight of Louie's face as Idaho Taylor jogged outside to join in the boys' football game. Her little brother looked gobsmacked.

Then she saw Crystal.

Unnoticed by Mimi, the Pomeranian had run outside. Her tail was wagging in a feathery white blur as she sniffed the grass. She chased the ball, jumping and twisting around and having what looked like the best time of her life.

Bella choked back a giggle. Crystal was heading for a large muddy patch in the middle of the grass as fast as her tiny legs could carry her. She tried to jump over, missed – and landed bottom first in the mud.

"Crystal!" Mimi gasped, stopping halfway through one of Amber's braids.

"Don't worry, Mimi," said Bella cheerfully. "It'll all come out in the wash!"

Top tips from vets!

Dogs come in many different sizes. Larger dogs will have different needs to those of smaller dogs, like a bigger bed, more space and bigger meals. But, whatever their size, all dogs have 5 main things they need to be healthy and happy. They are:

- Dogs need a comfy bed and safe area where they can play. They need things to keep them busy, like toys.

- A dog needs a healthy, balanced diet and lots of exercise so they don't become fat, as well as fresh water that they can drink at all times.

- Puppies need to be trained and get used to meeting people and other animals.

- Dogs need company and attention. Make sure that your dog is never left alone long enough for it to become distressed.

- Your dog will also need regular injections and treatments to prevent certain diseases or suffering from worms or fleas.

Did you know?

Dogs need lots of exercise. More active breeds will need at least two good walks every day.

For more tips on pet care, great competitions and games visit www.pdsa.org.uk/petprotectors

pdsa

for pets in need of vets

Dream Dogs

CHARLIE

Animal-crazy Bella is so excited to discover the headmistress of her school has a dog and is desperate to catch a glimpse of the mysterious pooch!

Bella gets a big surprise when her wish comes true and Mrs Frost brings Charlie to Dream Dogs, her mum's trendy grooming parlour, for a pampering session.

But there's an even bigger shock in store when Bella's younger brother plays a very naughty trick at the school fund-raiser, held to raise money for a new assembly hall, with very colourful consequences!

Read on for a sneak preview of the next Dream Dogs adventure...

Outside the classroom window, Bella could see the sea glinting behind the playground. She rested her chin on her hand and stared dreamily at the view. There were just two weeks of term until the summer holidays. Soon, she and her mum, her little brother, Louie, and their dog, Pepper, would all be on Sandmouth beach, having picnics and ice-creams and staying out late every evening. Bella hoped it would be a hot summer. It would be typical if the sun stopped shining in exactly two weeks's time.

"Bella?" said Mrs Frost.

Bella looked around in surprise. "Me?" she said.

Mrs Frost, the head teacher at Cliffside Primary, made a tutting noise. Mrs Frost had white hair and an icy gaze. The children called her Frosty.

"Yes, Bella," Mrs Frost said, raising her white eyebrows. "You. What ideas have you brought to the Summer Fair Committee?"

Bella tried to concentrate. She stared at the piece of paper in front of her. She'd drawn a picture of her dog Pepper. It was a lovely picture. She was pleased at how she'd drawn Pepper's rough brown head and big dark eyes. But it wasn't very helpful right now. What had her class asked Bella to say?

"Well," Bella said nervously. "It's Cliffside Primary's fiftieth anniversary this year, and... um...."

The other children at the meeting giggled.

Mrs Frost sighed. "Yes," she said. "We know that. We have lots of things in place for the anniversary. But what ideas have your class had?"

It was no good. Bella couldn't remember. She was going to have to make it up.

"A dog show," she blurted out. "With... prizes for the waggiest tail, and... um... the smiliest face and... the wettest tongue..."

Bella knew she was rambling. But to her amazement, Mrs Frost started nodding.

"A lovely idea," said Mrs Frost. "We could charge a pound for people to enter. I shall bring my dog along."

Bella blinked. Mrs Frost had a dog? She'd never seen Mrs Frost out walking a dog. It was a weird thought.

"What kind of dog have you got, Miss?" asked Bella's best friend, Amber.

"A Labradoodle, called Charlie," said Mrs Frost.

Bella frowned. She assumed Mrs Frost must have said 'Labrador' and she'd just misheard her. She was about to put her hand up to ask, but someone called out, "A labrabooble! What's that?"

Before Mrs Frost could answer, Amber cried, "No, silly, she said 'dabydoodle'!" and the whole class started laughing.

"OK children, settle down." Mrs Frost said, raising her hand to get the class to be quiet. "Charlie is a Labradoodle, which is a cross between a Labrador and a poodle. It's quite a rare breed so it's no wonder that you haven't heard of it before."

Bella's mouth opened with surprise – she had never heard of such a funny-sounding name for a dog, and couldn't wait to meet him!

Then and there, Bella decided she would *have* to find a way to get Mrs Frost to bring Charlie to Dream Dogs…

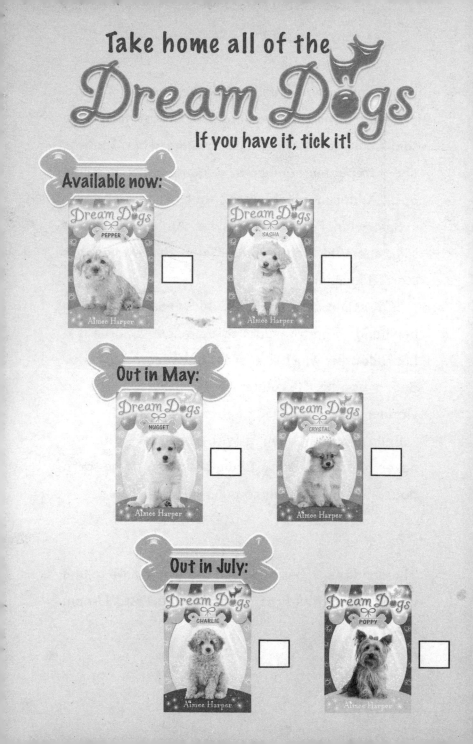